A DIXIE MORRIS ANIMAL ADVENTURE

DIXIE & JUMBO

GILBERT

MOODY PRESS
CHICAGO

©1998 by
GILBERT MORRIS

ISBN: 0-8024-3363-4

1 3 5 7 9 10 8 6 4 2

Printed in the United States of America

To my Boppa—
the most important man in my life.
I love you so much!
Thank you for everything you
have done for me.—Dixie Morris

CONTENTS

1
A SAD GOOD-BYE

Dixie Morris was ten years old. But the night her parents left for Africa, she felt more like a baby than anything else.

The little town of Milo had not seen many missionaries. All day long the house was filled with people. They had come to say good-bye to Dixie's parents.

Brother Stone was the pastor of the little church in Milo. Right in the middle of lunch, he stopped eating fried chicken long enough to say, "It must be hard for you to go so far away and leave Dixie here in this country."

Everyone looked at Dixie. She was sitting between her father and mother. Her father put his hand on her shoulder. It felt big and warm, and Dixie wanted to get in his lap.

"It *is* hard, Brother Stone," Dixie's father said. "We'll miss our girl very much. And she'll miss us."

"Daddy, couldn't I *please* go with you?" Dixie pleaded. "I wouldn't be any trouble at all."

Her mother let her hand fall on Dixie's other shoulder. She had blonde hair and blue eyes, just like Dixie's. "Oh, Dixie, we know you wouldn't be any trouble!"

"Of course not," her father said quickly. "But the place where we're going isn't very safe right now. It's no place for a little girl."

Brother Stone said, "Well, now, it's very nice of the Snyders to let Dixie live with them till you come back."

Roy Snyder was a distant relative of Dixie's father. He was a big man with a red face and not much hair. He said, "Edith and I are glad to help. But we've never had any children, so we don't know much about little girls."

His wife, Edith, was as thin as her husband was fat. She looked over her glasses at Dixie. "That's right," she said. "Roy and I aren't young anymore. And some children are so loud."

Mrs. Morris patted Dixie's shoulder. "Dixie isn't loud, Aunt Edith. She'll be good company for you."

Dixie saw that the Snyders were not very happy about having her. They tried not to show it, but she could tell.

Then the meal was over, and all the visitors were gone.

Dixie hoped that her parents would take her someplace where they could be alone. But they had the last of their packing to do. So she spent the rest of the day outside.

She walked around the farm, feeling sorry for herself. It had been fun living on a farm for a while. She had loved to gather the eggs. Now she just passed by the henhouse and said, "Who wants those old eggs, anyway?"

Every day she had visited the litter of pigs. She had named every one of them. Nathaniel was the smallest. She reached over the fence and picked him up.

"You'll be my friend, won't you, Nathaniel?" she whispered in his ear.

He nibbled at her neck.

Dixie played with the pigs for a time. Then she went down the path to the pond.

Shep, the collie dog, followed her. He'd been chasing the ducks. Now he came back and put his long nose right in her face.

She put her arms around his neck. "Oh, Shep!" she sobbed. "Why do they have to go off and leave me?"

Shep couldn't answer, of course. But he began to whine. It was as if he were saying, "Don't cry, Dixie. It'll be all right."

Just then Dixie heard someone coming. She pushed Shep away and wiped the tears from her eyes. But when she looked around, she saw that it wasn't her father, as she'd hoped. It was only Candy Sweet, the Snyder's hired hand. He was a big man, and he had hair as blonde as Dixie's and eyes as blue.

When Dixie first came to the farm, she'd tried to make friends with Candy. But he'd never said a word to her except "Hello."

He had a fishing pole in one hand and a can of worms in the other. He fished in the pond almost every day. Dixie had wanted to ask him to let her fish too. But she never had.

"Hello," she said as he took a worm out of his can.

He looked at her as if he'd never seen her before. Then he said, "Hello," and threw out the line and sat down.

Dixie stood and watched the red cork bob up and down in the water. *I wish he'd let me catch a fish,* she thought. But Candy didn't even look at her. So she left the pond and walked back toward the house.

She went inside, and her father saw her.

"Well—here you are!" he said. He came over and hugged her. "You promised to show me where the bird's nest is."

Dixie was glad to be with him. "Let's go right now," she said.

"Can I come too?" her mother asked with a smile.

That made it even better! The three of them left the house, and Dixie led them to the apple orchard. Someone had made a birdhouse and nailed it to a tree. "There it is!" Dixie cried. "If we watch, the mama bird will bring the baby birds something to eat."

They waited, and, sure enough, soon a bird came with a dragonfly in her beak. "That's the mama bird, I think," Dixie said. "When she leaves, we can go see the babies."

Soon the mother flew away.

Dixie's mother said, "They are beautiful birds. In a few more days the last two little ones will be gone, won't they?"

That suddenly made Dixie sad. "Yes. I won't have them to look at anymore." A tear ran down her cheek. "They won't have any mother or father—and neither will I."

Mrs. Morris gave her husband a quick look and said, "Come on, sweetheart, let's sit down over there by that old fence."

They sat on the grass, and her mother took her hand. "I know it's hard, especially for a little girl. But your father and I believe that God has told us to go. And we believe that He'll take care of all of us."

"Yes," her father said. "And it won't be forever. As soon as the danger is over, we'll come back and get you. Then we'll all be together again."

"But why can't I stay with Aunt *Sarah?*" Sarah Logan was her mother's sister.

"Aunt Sarah is finishing up her college work," her mother said. "She doesn't have any place to keep a little girl. And if she did, she's in class all day, so you'd be all alone."

"I'll be all alone here," Dixie said. "I don't have a single friend!"

"Then you must ask Jesus to give you a friend," her father said. "He can do anything."

They sat under the tree for a long time. Her parents tried to make her feel better. But Dixie was already dreading the moment when they'd get on the plane and leave.

Finally her father said, "Our plane leaves at five o'clock. We've got to go to the airport, Dixie."

He got to his feet, and Dixie asked, "Will you carry me on your back to the house? Like you used to when I was a little girl?"

He smiled and stooped down. "Jump on."

She got on, and he ran back to the house. It was fun, but as soon as he put her down, Uncle Roy came out and said, "Better get to the airport."

Dixie watched as the bags were put in the trunk. Then everyone got into the car. Uncle Roy drove. Dixie sat in back with her father and mother. She held tightly to their hands all the way.

At the airport, she saw that the big plane was ready to leave soon.

"Good-bye, Dixie," her mother whispered. "It won't be long. I love you."

Her father picked her up and kissed her. His own eyes were bright with tears. She held to his neck with both arms. Finally he pulled them away and said, "We'll all have to pray that Jesus will put us all together again."

Then they left to get on the plane.

Dixie stood and watched their plane take off. She watched until it was just a tiny dot. And then even that was gone.

"Come on, Dixie," Uncle Roy said. "It's time to go home."

But all the way back to the farm Dixie was thinking, *It's not my home. I don't have a home. And I don't have a single friend!*

2
FRIENDS ARE HARD TO FIND

A week after her father and mother left for Africa, Aunt Edith came in from the mailbox and said, "Here's a letter from your parents."

Dixie grabbed the letter and stared at it.

"Do you want me to read it to you?"

"No, ma'am. I can read it myself. I think I'll go outside and read it."

Dixie wanted to be alone with her letter, so she went down to the pond. She sat on a log in the shade of the oak tree and looked at the envelope. "Maybe it will say that I can come now and live with them."

She took a deep breath and opened the letter. She read through it as quickly as she could. Her mother told her about the trip to Africa. The last paragraph said:

Your father and I live in a very small room in a tiny house. There's no bathroom. There's no place to wash clothes. We don't mind, because we're doing it for Jesus. But it would be too hard for a little girl. We love you very much. Someday the Lord will let us all live together again.

Dixie was very sad. She put the letter back in the envelope. She tried not to cry. "I don't like it here on the farm. It's hard to find a friend."

But then she heard Aunt Edith's bell ring. She knew it wasn't lunchtime. But her aunt rang the bell whenever she wanted Dixie to come in from play. She got up and went to the house.

"Dixie," Aunt Edith said, "Sheriff Peck is here."

Sheriff Peck was a tall man with black hair. "Hello, Dixie," he said. "Would you like to go to a party?"

"What kind of a party?"

"Why, it's my boy Ollie's birthday," Sheriff Peck said. "Come along. I'll bring you back when it's over."

"I don't have a present to give him," Dixie said.

"Oh, that's all right," the sheriff said. "He won't expect you to give him one."

"You go along now," Aunt Edith said. "You're always saying you don't have any friends. Now you've been invited to a fine party."

"I'll go put on a clean dress."

"Oh, that dress is fine," Sheriff Peck said. He looked at his watch. He shook his head. "We'd better go."

Dixie went out and got into the sheriff's car. On the way, she asked, "How many children will be at the party?"

"Oh, about ten, I think."

Dixie thought, *I'll bet I'll find someone to be my friend at the party. Maybe a little girl about my age. She could come and visit me. She could stay overnight. Then I could go spend the night with her. We could be very good friends.*

She thought about that all the way to the party. And she asked the Lord to give her a friend. By the time Sheriff Peck pulled into the driveway, she felt sure that would happen.

19

"Come along, Dixie. I think the children are out in the backyard."

Dixie followed him. When they got there, she saw several boys and girls gathered around a table.

A boy with black hair was opening presents. He looked up and said, "Dad, you've missed the best part of the party."

"Sorry, Ollie," Sheriff Peck said. "But I'm here now. This is Dixie Morris. Dixie, this is Ollie. And this is my daughter, Patti. You can introduce her to all the other children, Patti."

A frown crossed Ollie's face. He shook his head. He said a little angrily, "Not right now, Patti. It's present-opening time."

Ollie began opening presents again. There were about ten of them. He tore the wrappings off and threw them on the ground. He didn't seem to like any of the presents very much.

And Dixie noticed that he didn't say thank you.

Finally he opened the last one, a nice red fire truck. He looked at it, then put it on the table with the other gifts. And then he looked at Dixie. "Where's my present?"

Dixie felt awful! Everyone was staring

at her. She said, "I'm sorry, Ollie. I didn't have time to get you a present."

Ollie frowned. "I never heard of anyone going to a birthday party without taking a present!"

Sheriff Peck said, "Now, Ollie, you know we only thought about asking Dixie a little while ago."

Mrs. Peck nodded her head. "That's right. If she'd had time, Dixie would have brought a present like all the other children."

Ollie looked ready to argue, but Sheriff Peck said quickly, "It's about time for the ice cream and cake."

Everyone shouted. Mrs. Peck cleared the table while Sheriff Peck brought two big containers of ice cream out of the house. "We've got chocolate and vanilla," he said.

"And here's the cake," his wife announced. "You light the candles, Henry. And Ollie can blow them out."

Dixie watched Ollie blow out the candles.

Then Mrs. Peck handed out pieces of cake. Her husband dipped ice cream for them all.

Dixie kept waiting for one of the little girls to come and talk to her. But none of them did.

21

She took her paper plate and went to get her cake.

"So glad you could come, Dixie," Mrs. Peck said. "You must come and see Ollie and Patti again. I know you must be lonesome with your mother and father so far away."

She was right about that!

As the party went on, Dixie felt more and more alone. All the other children knew one another. They talked and laughed loudly. Patti was talking to two other girls. Dixie moved closer, hoping they would be friendly.

But Patti just looked at her and said, "There's more ice cream if you want it." Then she went back to talking to the other girls. And none of the other boys and girls talked to her.

"Sheriff Peck, would you take me home?" she asked.

The sheriff stared at her. He looked at the other children. "Why, the party's just getting started, Dixie. You ought to stay and make friends."

Dixie blinked back the tears. "Take me home, please."

He tried to persuade her to stay, but she didn't want to. Finally he took her home.

As she got out of the sheriff's car, he said, "Children aren't always kind, Dixie. I'll have a talk with Ollie and Patti."

Dixie said, "Thank you for bringing me home."

Then she went down to the pond and sat on her log. Shep followed her, and Mr. Beak, the duck, stared at her with his yellow eyes.

She put her arms around the dog's neck and whispered, "Friends are hard to find, Shep."

3

CANDY ISN'T SWEET

Maybe Dixie will be able to make friends when school starts."

Dixie had been digging worms in the soft ground under the kitchen window. She stopped when she heard her Uncle Roy's voice. It wasn't nice to listen to other people talk, but she couldn't help it.

"Well, I certainly hope so," Aunt Edith said. "That child is about to drive me crazy. I've been wondering if we did the right thing letting them leave her with us."

"Oh, she's a good child," Uncle Roy said quickly. "No trouble at all, really."

"No trouble!" Aunt Edith sniffed. "Why, Roy, I wear my legs down to the ankles taking care of that child. You know I do!"

Dixie saw a fat worm wiggling in a clump of black dirt. She reached out to pick it up. As she tugged at it, her uncle said, "She misses her parents. And she's more lonesome than sick."

Dixie got up, being very quiet. She heard her aunt saying, "I'm just too nervous to keep a child. You know my nerves."

"I ought to," Uncle Roy said sharply. "I've been hearing about them for thirty years."

Dixie started to walk away. She heard him add, "The child's just plain lonesome. I think when school starts and she makes friends, she'll be all right."

Dixie thought about that as she went down the path toward the pond. She went to where the water was deep and picked up the pole Uncle Roy had gotten her. She baited her hook. She threw out her line. The red-and-white cork settled beside a green lily pad. She sat down and waited for a fish to bite.

Soon the cork began to tremble. She watched it. When it went down with a *plop,* she jerked the pole. Her heart always beat faster when that happened. When she saw the fish, she cried out, "I've got you!"

She lifted the fish onto the land. And then came the hardest part. The fish flopped around, trying to get back into the water. He was beautiful. He had green stripes and a red spot on his side. She took the hook out and put him in a tin bucket with holes punched in it. Then she put the bucket back in the water. That way the fish would stay alive until she was ready to go.

She fished for more than an hour. Then she went back toward the house.

She found Candy beside the woodpile. He was splitting wood.

She said, "Candy, would you clean the fish I caught, please?"

As usual, he said nothing. He put down the ax and followed her to the backyard.

She held up the string of fish, saying, "I caught seven. Look, this one has a red spot. Isn't he pretty?"

Candy looked at the fish. He said, "It's a redear perch."

He spoke so little that Dixie was surprised. She tried to make him talk some more. As he took the fish off the stringer, she said, "Maybe you could teach me how to clean fish. Then you wouldn't have to do it all the time."

He looked at her and grunted. Then he picked up one of the fish.

She guessed the grunt meant yes. But it could just as easily have meant, "You could never learn to clean fish." She watched as he took the big knife.

He cut off the fish's head. He cleaned away the insides. Then he said, "You can take the scales off." He took the fish and a spoon and showed her how.

When she tried it, the scales began to flake off.

"Oh, this is easy!" she cried. She finished the fish and put it in a pan of water. She scaled the other six fish. "I like to learn to do new things," she said. "Where did you learn to clean fish, Candy?"

He looked at her, then shook his head. "Don't know." He washed his hands and moved away.

She heard the sound of his ax and said, "Not all candy is sweet. I wish he'd talk more."

They ate the fish for supper. They were delicious. Aunt Edith was grouchy, but she was a good cook.

After they finished eating, Dixie helped with the dishes. Candy went to his room, which was a little shack outside the house.

Uncle Roy read the paper. Then he went outside too.

Just as Dixie and her aunt were finishing the dishes, she heard a car drive up. Dixie looked out the window. "It's Sheriff Peck," she said.

They went outside and found the sheriff talking to Uncle Roy.

Sheriff Peck was saying, "You better keep your eyes open, Roy. Can't tell about a thing like this."

"What's the matter, Sheriff?" Aunt Edith asked.

"Why, we've got some kind of a thief," he said. "Just wanted to warn you to keep watch."

"What sort of stuff has he stolen, Sheriff?" Uncle Roy asked.

Sheriff Peck took off his hat. He scratched his head. He looked a little puzzled. "Well, it's sort of strange. Mostly he's taken *food.* Over at James Robinson's place, he took a sack of apples. But he *didn't* take a brand-new radio that was right beside them. Most crooks would have taken that radio."

"Is food all he takes?" Uncle Roy asked.

"That's mostly it. Lots of vegetables, I hear. But he sure does make some funny choices. He could have taken some of Angie Willis's fresh-baked pies. They was all out in the summer house. But he passed them up and took a half bale of hay."

"He took *hay* instead of Angie Willis's pies?" Uncle Roy asked. "Must be crazy—a man can't eat *hay!*"

Sheriff Peck nodded. "Could be. And we don't want any crazy men loose in our county." He looked around. Then he lowered his voice. "Roy, I got an idea. Some of the folks around here have always thought your hired man was a little bit crazy."

Uncle Roy stared at him. "Candy? Why, he wouldn't steal food. He gets all he can eat right here at our table."

"That's what I thought," Sheriff Peck said. "But the thing is, all the stealing has been done right around here. It's like your place is kind of the center of it. And Candy Sweet *is* peculiar. You have to admit that."

Dixie listened as the men talked. She wondered if it was so. She had never liked Candy. He was so big and strong and hardly ever said anything. But she had never thought of him as a thief.

Finally Uncle Roy said, "Well, I'll keep

an eye on Candy, Sheriff. But I think you're barking up the wrong tree."

"Most all the stealing takes place at night," the sheriff said. "So you just be sure he's not roaming around. May not be him, though."

That night Dixie lay awake a long time thinking about the thief. And she hoped it wasn't Candy Sweet.

4
A MYSTERIOUS STRANGER

The whole countryside was buzzing about the thief.

When Dixie went to church Sunday, she overheard a large lady talking to Pastor Stone. The lady said, "You mark my words, Pastor. It may only be food he's stealing *now*, but the thief won't be satisfied with that!"

Later, when they were on the way home, she asked, "Uncle Roy, do you think Candy is the thief?"

"No, I don't," he said. "I've been watching him pretty close, too."

After lunch Aunt Edith said, "You do your homework before you take a nap, Dixie."

School had started, but it wasn't like Dixie had hoped it would be. She had to ride a bus for a long way. A girl named

Carla was friendly, but Dixie saw her only at school. It wasn't like having a *real* friend.

She worked on her homework, took a nap, and then wrote a long letter to her parents. She told them all about the mysterious thief who was stealing from everyone. But she said, "I don't care if Candy doesn't talk much. I don't think he's a thief."

She finished her letter. Then she went downstairs just in time for supper. After she helped with the dishes, she said, "Can I go down to the pond, Aunt Edith?"

"I suppose so—but don't bring any fish back. I don't want to clean them."

"I'm just going for a walk," Dixie said.

The sky was getting dark as she left the house. Most of the animals were asleep. The pond was quiet, and she sat beside it for a long time. She thought, *It's getting late. I better go back to the house.*

But then she caught a glimpse of something moving just across the pond. At first she thought it was an animal. She sat very still and slowly turned her head. And then she saw that it was not an animal—it was a man!

He was wearing dark clothes. He had a soft hat pulled over his eyes. He was standing beside a big tree—watching *her!* She couldn't see his eyes, but she knew he was looking at her. It was so dark that if he had not moved, she never would have seen him. Now he stood still.

Dixie's heart began to beat very fast. She had never seen him before. He wasn't a neighbor. No neighbor would hide in the dark as this man was doing.

She wanted to run as fast as she could. But she forced herself to get up and walk at a normal pace. The woods were so quiet she could hear the sound of her footsteps very clearly. She looked back once. But it was so black, she could see nothing. Once she thought she heard steps, but she didn't stop.

All the way home she kept on saying the special Bible verse she had learned. And when she got to the yard, she took a deep breath. "He didn't get me," she whispered. "Thank You, Jesus!"

She stood on the porch for a while but never saw anything. Finally she went inside and went to bed.

That night Dixie dreamed about a man dressed in black. She woke up once, afraid. But then she remembered that the Lord had kept her safe. She said her verse again, "The Lord will protect you from all evil."

But she knew the man wasn't Candy Sweet.

The next morning at breakfast, Candy came in late. He said, "Somebody took some of the potatoes out of the barn last night."

Everybody stared at him.

Uncle Roy said, "How do you know, Candy?"

"Had some of them up in the loft. Went up to turn them so they won't spoil."

"And they were gone?" Aunt Edith asked nervously.

"About a bushel, I guess." He began to eat his breakfast.

Uncle Roy said, "I'll have to call Sheriff Peck and tell him about this. Sure do hate to hear it. When you count it up, there's been a *lot* of food stolen. No one man could eat that much. He must be selling it."

Dixie was waiting for him to ask her if *she* had seen anything. She was ready to tell him about the man who'd been watching her. But he got busy with his call to the sheriff.

She thought, *I'll tell Sheriff Peck when he gets here.*

But Sheriff Peck didn't come that day. And when she finally *did* see the sheriff, it was too late to tell.

5

THE MYSTERY IS SOLVED

Dixie came awake with a start. She had gone to bed early on a Thursday evening. But she woke up when she heard loud voices. She got out of bed and ran to the window.

In the dim morning light she saw her uncle and Candy standing in the yard, holding onto somebody.

She dressed quickly and ran down the stairs.

She found Aunt Edith in the doorway. She tried to squeeze by, but Aunt Edith said, "Dixie! What are you doing out of bed this early?"

"Who's out there?"

"It's the thief, that's who it is," Aunt Edith said. "Your Uncle Roy set a trap. And now they've got him!"

They brought the man to the house.

"Move back, Edith," Uncle Roy said. He pushed his way inside, and Dixie saw that he was holding the arm of a very young man.

"I'll take him in to the sheriff's office," her uncle said.

"How'd you catch him?" Aunt Edith asked.

As Uncle Roy explained, Dixie looked at the thief. He was about fifteen. He was thin. He held a soft hat in his hand, and his hair was long and black. It needed not only cutting but also washing, she decided. He had a narrow, dark face and a pair of dark eyes. At first she'd thought he was a full-grown man. But though he was tall, he was just a boy. He looked scared.

He looked hard at Dixie.

She blinked. He seemed to be trying to tell her something. And then she thought, *He's the one who was watching me at the pond!*

Uncle Roy finished his story. "So Candy and me, we took turns watching the barn. I knew he'd come back for more potatoes— and he did."

"Well, I hope you know what's going to happen to you, young man," Aunt Edith said. "You won't be doing any more stealing for a while. No sir. You'll be in jail!"

The boy didn't even look at her. He was still looking at Dixie.

She wanted to ask why he had been watching her, but it was too late.

Uncle Roy asked, "What's your name, boy?"

"Chad Taylor," the boy said.

"Chad, if you were hungry, we'd have fed you. But you couldn't have eaten all you stole. Who'd you sell it to?"

Chad shrugged his thin shoulders. He didn't answer.

Uncle Roy said sadly, "Hate to see a young fellow get off on the wrong track. Well, we've got no choice. Edith, get this boy something to eat."

Aunt Edith said, "You feed him yourself." Then she went off upstairs.

Uncle Roy had Chad sit at the table. He gave him a plate of leftovers from supper last night. "Might as well eat, boy," he said. "You want some pie and milk, Dixie?"

She thought she was too excited to eat. But she sat down. While Chad ate and while the men drank coffee, she ate a piece of pie.

Chad Taylor said nothing. But he ate hungrily and asked politely for a cup of coffee.

Candy brought it to him.

Then Uncle Roy said, "I'll go warm up the car."

When he was gone, Dixie watched the boy.

He sat quiet for a long time, then asked, "Your name is Dixie?"

"Yes."

He sipped his coffee and seemed to think about that. "You like to go to the pond and fish, don't you?"

"Oh yes. I go there a lot."

"I'm surprised a girl like you doesn't spend more time with her friends."

Dixie said, "Well, I don't really have any friends."

That seemed to mean something to him. He looked over at Candy.

The big man had his back to them. He was watching to see when Uncle Roy came with the car.

"You mean—you don't have even *one* friend?"

"No, I really don't." Dixie heard the car start. At the same time she heard Aunt

Edith coming down the stairs. Her heels made a loud noise.

Dixie had been working on her writing last night. Her red tablet was still on the table.

Suddenly Chad picked up the tablet and a pencil. He wrote something on one of the pages. Then he tore out the page and handed it to Dixie.

"Don't read it until I'm gone," he whispered.

Dixie stuck the paper in the pocket of her blue jeans.

Aunt Edith came into the kitchen. At the same time, the car horn sounded. Candy got up. He waited for Chad to do the same.

Dixie looked at Chad, who was watching her, and she gave him a little nod.

He got up at once and went outside.

Dixie went to the door. She watched the car leave the driveway.

Aunt Edith said, "My nerves are so bad! I'm going to my room and lie down."

"I don't feel like going to school today, Aunt Edith. May I stay home?"

"Yes, I guess so. Too much excitement. But you'll have to take care of yourself. I'm going to lie down until my nerves get calm."

She went upstairs.

Candy looked back at Dixie. "Got work to do."

Dixie said, "He didn't look like a thief, did he, Candy?"

"I don't know." He shrugged. "Don't know what a thief looks like."

Candy left, and Dixie stood there almost trembling. She took the piece of paper from her pocket and stared at it. She knew better. She knew that what she had done would make Aunt Edith mad. She knew that she ought to give the note to Sheriff Peck. *It might be evidence,* she thought.

But then she opened the paper and read what Chad had written. It was scribbled so badly she could hardly read it. And, besides, she had crumpled the paper to get it into her pocket. She laid it down on the table to smooth it out. Finally she made out the words, which were printed in big letters:

GO OUT TO THE OLD PECAN GROVE PAST THE POND. YOU'LL FIND A FRIEND THERE.

There were a few more words. They were so scrawled that she had to study them for a long time. Finally she made them out and read them out loud:

DON'T BE AFRAID.

She read the note over and over. She knew where the old grove was. Her uncle had once said it was about a mile past the pond. He'd told her, "We'll get us some good pecans when they fall." And he'd pointed in that direction. But she had never been there.

Again and again she read the words:

YOU'LL FIND A FRIEND THERE.

Suddenly a thought came to her. *What if there's another thief out there? Maybe he'll kidnap me and make them turn Chad loose!*

The thought scared her. But the note had said, "Don't be afraid." Back came the words that had made her want to go to the grove in the first place: "You'll find a friend there."

Dixie washed the dishes. Then she

went to her room and put on her old clothes. She was ready to go, when she thought, *This may be dangerous!*

She went back and knelt beside her bed and prayed.

6
DIXIE FINDS A FRIEND

Dixie sat down at the kitchen table again. She was trying to make up her mind. Once she almost tore up the note. But she kept remembering the look in Chad's eyes. Finally she got up, saying to herself, *I practically promised him I'd go.* But she knew that wasn't so either.

"Well—I just *want* to go," she said at last. "I want a friend. If there's one in that grove, I'm going to find him!"

Something didn't feel right. She knew it was probably wrong not to tell her aunt and uncle, but . . .

She left the house and ran past the pond. She took a path that led through a big field. It was thick with weeds and briars. Soon her legs were cut and scratched.

She came out of the field at last and

into a woods. She started walking through the trees. The farther she went, the more nervous she became.

I don't even know what a pecan tree looks like, she thought.

Deeper and deeper into the woods she went. Once she crossed a deep ravine with a small creek at the bottom. Then she saw something over to her left. It looked like an old building. She remembered what her uncle had said. There was an old barn by the pecan grove. "Used to be a house too, but it burned down," he had told her.

She came into a clearing, and there it was—a barn. Much of the roof was off. The siding boards were mostly off too. Maybe about half of it was still standing.

"How could I find a friend way out here?" she asked herself. "Nobody would live in an old place like that!"

She wanted to go home. But she was curious. "I've come this far," she said. "I might as well look around."

She went close to the barn and called, "Is anyone here?" Her voice sounded hollow.

But no one answered.

She took a deep breath and slipped

inside. It was cool and darkish, but sunlight came in through the spaces left by the missing boards.

Dixie walked around, a little afraid. But she soon saw that nobody was in the barn.

"I wonder what's up in the loft."

She climbed the ladder and saw at once that someone had been staying there! There was a bed made out of straw. There was a lamp on a box. On a nail hung two shirts and a pair of pants.

"Why, this is where *Chad's* been staying!" Dixie said. She looked around. She saw two apples and half a loaf of bread. There was a notebook too, and she picked it up. But it was too dark to read here. She took it with her when she left the loft.

Going out into the sunlight, she could see that the notebook was some sort of diary. There were dates on the pages. But it was written so poorly that it was hard to make out.

"He can't write as well as he can print," Dixie said to herself.

She was really thirsty by then and decided to go back to the creek and get a drink.

I don't think there's any friend here,

she thought. *But I'll take the notebook to Chad. He'll probably want to keep it.*

She crossed under the trees to the brook. It was not far from the barn. She bent down and took a long drink of water. It was so good. It was sweet and pure—better than any soda pop.

She sat down and studied the notebook. About all she could make out was that Chad was running away from something. She didn't know what he was running away from, though. And there was someone with him. He kept saying things such as "He got pretty hungry today" and "I hope he doesn't get sick." Several times he said, "If they get him, they'll kill him!"

"I wonder who *he* is?" Dixie said. "And why would anybody want to kill him?"

She thought about it. She read a little more. It was very warm, but the breeze under the trees was cool. Dixie began to get sleepy. Her eyes drooped. Finally she put the notebook in her pocket. She said, "I'll just rest a few minutes before I start back." Almost at once she dropped off into sleep.

When she started waking up again, a fly was crawling over her hair. She raised her hand to brush it away. But her hand didn't hit a fly. It touched something much larger than a fly.

She was still half asleep, but she rolled over to see if she had touched a branch of a tree.

It was all a little puzzling, for it seemed much darker than it should have been. *I can't have slept until dark!* she thought. She was confused and brushed at the fly again as she opened her eyes.

For one moment she lay there not able to believe what she was seeing. Then she let out a squeak and tried to sit up.

Right there, with his trunk almost touching her, stood THE BIGGEST ELEPHANT SHE HAD EVER SEEN!

He was blocking the sun (that was why it seemed darker). And she could see his tiny eyes watching her.

Dixie had never been so scared in all her life! She was sure that he was going to pick her up with that huge trunk and dash her to the ground. Or else he was going to just lift his foot and step on her.

Slowly she drew up her feet, then pushed herself until she was sitting.

The elephant stood watching. He was

swaying from side to side, and he kept his trunk up.

He is smelling me! Dixie thought suddenly. She got to her feet but knew that it was hopeless to run. *He'd catch me before I took ten steps.*

She was beginning to hope, though. She was thinking that if he'd been going to hurt her, he'd have already done it.

She took one step backward—then waited.

The elephant watched her out of his little eyes but made no other move.

She took another step back, then another.

Still he just watched.

Finally she turned and began to walk away. She was almost afraid to breathe. She expected to hear his huge feet pounding the earth behind her. But she didn't hear a sound.

Dixie's curiosity got the better of her. She stopped and turned around.

He was still there, just watching.

Somehow he looked very lonesome. She knew that animals liked company. Most of the animals on the farm came running to her. And all at once she thought, *Why, he's waiting for Chad to come back.*

That was it! She knew then what the notebook meant. The one that Chad kept calling "he" was this huge elephant.

And then she said out loud, "But Chad will never come back!"

The elephant's huge ears suddenly fanned out to catch the sound of her voice. He took one step forward and lifted his trunk. His eyes were still on her.

"You poor thing!" Dixie cried. She ran back to the elephant, all fear gone.

She put her hand out.

He touched it with his trunk, very gently.

She said, "Oh, dear! You've lost your only friend."

And then she understood what the note meant. "Chad must have seen how much I needed a friend," she said. "And he knew that you wouldn't have a friend either—not with him in jail!"

The elephant seemed to listen to her. He lifted his head as if he were nodding.

"Why, you understand what I'm saying, don't you?" Dixie cried in delight. "You're just like a big puppy, wanting someone to pay you attention."

Then she frowned. "And that's why Chad was stealing food. It was for you."

She was happy about that. It didn't seem so bad to take food for an animal that was hungry. But then another thought came.

Now that Chad's in jail, who'll take care of you?

The elephant moved his ears forward. He touched her cheek with the tip of his trunk.

"I'll take you back with me," she said. She smiled, but not for long. She suddenly remembered what she had read in Chad's diary. *If they catch him, they'll kill him.*

"No!" she said. She reached up and held his trunk in her arms. "I can't let them kill you!"

She knew it was time to go back to Uncle Roy's. She said, "I've got to go now. But I'll be back with something for you to eat. You wait here."

He seemed to listen to her. He didn't try to follow.

When she was at the edge of the field, she looked back and saw his huge shadow. He lifted his trunk. And for the first time she heard the trumpet call of an African elephant. It was not loud, and it seemed very sad.

Dixie turned and ran toward the house, but she was happy.

I've got a real friend! she was thinking. *A real friend of my very own!*

7

CHAD ASKS
A FAVOR

Dixie thought of a plan. Every Saturday morning Uncle Roy and Aunt Edith went to town to buy groceries. When they got to town next time, she said, "Could I play in the park while you're getting the groceries?"

Uncle Roy said, "Of course. We'll pick you up when we get through."

She knew the sheriff's office was on the square, right across from the park. She went there first. She'd never been in his office, but the sheriff was in, sitting at a desk.

He got up with a smile on his face. "Well, this is a surprise," he said. "You're not in town all alone, are you?"

"No sir. Uncle Roy and Aunt Edith are buying groceries."

"So you decided to pay me a visit?"

Dixie said, "Well, I'd like to see Chad. I thought he might like some cookies."

Sheriff Peck stroked his chin and thought hard. "I suppose it will be all right. Come along and bring your cookies." He took a big key from his desk, walked across the room, and opened a door.

Dixie followed him. She saw a hall with cells on both sides.

The sheriff led her to one of the cells and said, "Chad, you've got a visitor."

He unlocked the cell door for her, saying, "Just give me a call when you're ready to leave, Dixie."

Dixie waited until the sheriff had left and then held out the bag. "I brought you some chocolate chip cookies."

Chad suddenly smiled and took it. "Well, thanks a lot, Dixie."

"Are they going to keep you in jail for a long time?"

"I guess so." He ate a cookie, then looked at her. "Did you read the note I gave you?"

"Yes, and I went out to the old pecan grove too."

Chad stared at her. He said, "That was

pretty brave. Did you—did you see any-thing?"

Dixie nodded and gave him a big smile. Her eyes were bright with excitement as she told him about her trip. She said, "I was so afraid when I woke up. But after a while I wasn't afraid anymore. He's very big but so gentle!"

"His name is Jumbo," Chad said. He had listened to her story carefully. Now he said, "I guess you wonder what in the world an elephant is doing in your woods."

Dixie pulled his notebook out of her pocket and handed it to him. "I found your notebook," she said. "I read part of it. What does the part mean that says, 'If they find him, they'll kill him'?"

Chad said, "I'll have to tell you the whole story. You see, I've been working with a circus. I ran away from a home for boys, and it was the only thing I could find to do. My job was taking care of the animals. And my favorite animal of all was Jumbo."

"He's a *circus* elephant?" Dixie asked. "Does he know any tricks?"

"Oh yes." Chad nodded. "But he's not like the ordinary circus elephant. Almost all trained elephants are from Asia. But Jumbo is an African elephant."

"What's the difference?"

"Well, for one thing, African elephants are much larger. And some people say that African elephants are not as gentle as the ones from other places. They say that they're likely to turn bad and kill somebody."

"Is that true?"

"I don't know about all elephants," Chad said. "But I know Jumbo is as gentle as a kitten. He wouldn't hurt a fly."

"I just *love* him, Chad," Dixie whispered. "But what are you doing here with Jumbo?"

"Oh," Chad said, "you see, Jumbo is getting old for an elephant. He's fifty-one years old. I heard the owner of the circus say that they were going to have to get a new elephant. And then I heard him say, 'We'll have to have old Jumbo put to sleep.'"

"You mean—*kill* him?" Dixie asked. Her eyes were as big as they could be. "They wouldn't kill him just because he's old, would they, Chad?"

"Yes, they would. They did that to an old lion just last month."

"But we can't let them do that!"

Chad said, "No, and that's why I ran away with him. The circus was in a little town about twenty miles from here. I found out that they were going to put Jumbo to sleep before they left. So I ran off in the middle of the night with him. They spent a few days looking for us, I guess. But we hid out in an old barn about like the one here. Since then we've been traveling at night to keep from being seen."

Dixie shook her head. "It's pretty hard to hide an elephant, isn't it?"

"You're telling me! Can't go very far in one night. Can't go close to any towns. And just keeping him fed is an awful job."

Dixie asked, "But what's going to happen to Jumbo? Now that you can't take care of him."

Chad bit his lip, looking very worried. "He'll die. Either he'll starve, or he'll wander into a town where they'll shoot him. Or the circus will send people to put him to sleep." He suddenly put his head down and wiped his eyes. "I—I did all I could to save him, Dixie. But I just couldn't do it!"

Dixie put her hand on his arm. "Don't

feel bad," she begged. "You did so much for Jumbo. And maybe it'll still be all right."

"No, it won't." Chad looked very angry. "Nothing ever comes out all right. In my whole life nothing's ever worked."

Dixie didn't know what to do. She finally said, "My mother and father say that the way to get things made right is to pray about them."

Chad shook his head and looked stubborn. "I don't believe any of that."

"Well, *I* do!" Dixie said. She wasn't too sure that she believed it as much as she should. But she wanted to believe it. And she wanted to cheer Chad up. "I'm going to pray that Jumbo will be all right."

"Pray all you please," Chad said. "I think *people* have to make things happen. I had a plan—but it's no good now."

Dixie asked. "What kind of a plan?"

"Oh, I've got an uncle who's got a big ranch in Arkansas. He's got lots of money, but he's real strange. I spent a summer working for him before my folks died. It was fun. But I wanted more excitement than watching cows all day long." Chad gave her a sad smile. "I've learned a few things since then. I've had enough excitement to last me for a long time. I'd like to get Jumbo to that ranch and then just work for my uncle."

"Why, that's a good plan!"

"Not really. Arkansas is too far."

"Maybe you ought to call him on the phone."

Chad gave her a funny look. "That's exactly what I wanted to do. But like I said, my uncle is strange. He doesn't like modern inventions very much. He won't have a television set on the place—and no telephone!"

"Chad, do you really think he'd help with Jumbo?"

"Sure. He's just odd enough to love the idea of having an elephant on his ranch." His eyes lit up. But then he frowned. "But it's all over now. I'm in jail, and that's it."

"I wish I could help," Dixie said. "I just love Jumbo."

"Well, there's still a chance." Chad pulled his chair up closer. "Dixie, if you could take care of Jumbo just for a while, it'd give me time to work on this thing. I could do it—I know I could!—if I just had a little time. Will you do it? Feed Jumbo until I can come up with an idea?"

Dixie looked at him with alarm. "But Chad, I'm only a girl! I wouldn't know how to feed an elephant. I wouldn't have any way to get the food to him."

He said, "Well, you said a minute ago you believe in asking God to help you do things. If you really meant it, you could ask Him to help you with this."

Dixie tried to think, but it was all too sudden. She finally said, "All right, Chad. I'll get something for Jumbo to eat today. And I'll ask Jesus to help."

"Great!" he cried. There was a hopeful light in his eyes.

Dixie got up and said, "I'll have to go now. I'll bring you something good to eat tomorrow."

Chad watched the sheriff escort Dixie out. Then he watched her through his barred window as she walked down the street.

"Well, Jumbo," he said, "there goes your only hope of staying alive!"

8

AN ANSWER TO PRAYER

Did you have a good time playing in the park, Dixie?" Uncle Roy asked as they drove home.

"Oh yes. It was very nice." Dixie waited a little while. Then she said, "I went to see Sheriff Peck first, Uncle Roy. And I took some cookies to Chad."

All the way home she tried to think of some way to get food out to Jumbo. They got home by noon. Since it was Saturday, Dixie didn't have to do any homework. While they were taking the groceries in, she got an idea.

"Would it be all right if I packed a lunch and went on a picnic?"

"I suppose so," Aunt Edith said. "But don't you stay too long."

"All right."

Dixie ran upstairs and put on her old clothes. She took the pillowcases off her pillows and rolled them into a ball. Then she put them in a sack. They were part of her plan.

After that she came downstairs and found that her aunt had a sack lunch ready for her. Dixie took the sack and ran out the front door. She put it in the small red wagon that she played with. She left the yard, pulling the wagon by a rope.

Shep followed her, and this time she let him come. He was part of her plan.

She went first to the small building that was used for the pigs' food. Her uncle had sorted all the bad apples from the orchard just a few days earlier. Dixie loaded the red wagon with apples. She filled the pillowcases too.

"Come here, Shep," she said. "You've got to help."

Shep came over, and she tied the wagon rope to his collar. "You've got to pull the wagon, Shep. We've got a long way to go."

It *was* a long way. More than once she had to stop and rest. They both got thirsty too. But finally she said, "Look, Shep—there's the barn. We're almost there."

Shep barked, as if to say, "Well, it's about *time!*"

As they walked up to the old farm building, Dixie said, "Now, Shep, you're going to see an elephant for the first time. Don't be afraid. He's very nice." She untied the rope on Shep's collar.

Shep barked again and wagged his tail. His eyes were bright. Now he seemed to be saying, "What—me be afraid?"

Dixie called out, "Jumbo! Jumbo! Where are you?"

The big front door slowly swung open. And there stood Jumbo.

Shep let out a shrill bark. Then he put his tail between his legs and ran away as fast as his legs would carry him.

Dixie had to laugh, though she felt a little sorry for him. "I guess any dog would be scared of Jumbo," she said.

Jumbo came out of the barn. He stretched out his trunk, and Dixie put her arms around it.

"Oh, poor Jumbo!" she cried. "I'll bet you've been lonesome, haven't you?"

She turned and picked up an apple from the wagon. "Here—see if you like this."

Jumbo reached out his trunk and took it from her hand as easily as could be. He tucked in his trunk and put the apple in his mouth.

Dixie saw him chewing on it, and then he put his trunk out again.

"Oh, you *do* like apples, don't you?" she cried. "Here, let me get you a lot of them."

She began to feed him, and he took the apples as fast as she could pick them up. "Jumbo, you're really hungry, aren't you?" she said. It was fun feeding an elephant. Finally the apples in the wagon were gone. "I've got some more in these pillowcases," she said.

Soon Jumbo had eaten all of those too and was still reaching for more.

"Jumbo, that's all I could bring!" she said. "And next time I might not be able to get Shep to come with me." Then she said, "Oh, I forgot. You can have my lunch."

She wasn't sure if elephants liked bacon and egg sandwiches and cookies. But she found out they did. Jumbo ate her lunch all in one bite.

He watched her, and she began to worry. "I'll never be able to feed you," she said out loud. "In the first place, there aren't many more apples. It's going to take a *lot* of food for you."

He nodded his big head.

She said, "And even if I had enough food, I couldn't get it here. I just don't know what to do!"

Dixie moved closer to the elephant until she stood right beside one of his huge front legs. It was as big as a small tree. There were calluses on his knees, she saw. She patted him on one knee. And when she tapped his knee, Jumbo raised his trunk and sat down!

Dixie jumped back, a bit afraid. But then she guessed why he had done that. "It's what you did in the circus, isn't it, Jumbo?"

He sat looking at her, and she said, "Do you mind if I go for a ride, Jumbo?"

He raised his trunk and made a trumpet sound.

Dixie pulled herself up on his knee, then onto his back. As soon as she was seated, he got up. It was scary, because his front end got up first. But she grabbed one of his ears and held on. When he was up on his four feet, the ground looked a long way down.

But she said, "Go on, Jumbo! Let's go!" And when she kicked him gently with her heels, he started walking.

What fun that was! It was the most fun she'd ever had in her whole life. Way up in the air, she could see for a long way. They swayed back and forth as he walked along. For more than an hour they walked around. She didn't know how to make him go where *she* wanted, but finally they came to the creek. Jumbo stopped for a drink of water. He just stuck his trunk in it and sucked it up.

When he had enough, he just stood there.

Dixie had an idea. She shouted, "Down, Jumbo! Get down!" And she tapped him on top of the head.

It worked! Jumbo swayed forward. When he was down, she slid off onto his knee, then to the ground. He got to his feet and looked at her.

"I've got to find some way to help you, Jumbo," she said. And she remembered that once her mother had told her, "If you can't think of a way to help yourself, Dixie—ask God to help you."

Dixie said, "Jumbo, you stay here. I've

74

got to go try and get help. I sure do wish *you* could pray!"

She turned and walked back to the barn. She got the wagon and started home. Jumbo stood watching, and she waved at him. "I'll be back, Jumbo. You just wait and see."

She made the trip back to the farm as fast as she could. All the way, she was thinking about what to do. And she was asking the Lord to help her.

When she got home, she found Candy. He was fastening wire to a post. He looked big and scary, and as usual he wasn't smiling. Dixie was afraid to ask him for help, but she knew she had to.

"Candy, there's something I can't do. I need someone to help me. It has to be someone big and strong—a grown-up person."

Candy stood there looking down at her. At first she thought he was going to ignore her. Then he said, "Well, what is it?"

She had it all thought out. "I can't tell you. I'll have to show you. Will you come with me?"

Candy just looked at her. He didn't say anything for a while. Then he said, "I guess so."

"Oh, Candy!" Dixie cried. "I'm so glad! Come on, now. We need to go on your tractor—and we need to take a bale of hay." She went up and took his hand. "Please, Candy. It's important."

He shrugged and said again, "I guess so."

They went to get his tractor. He hitched on a trailer, then threw a bale of hay on it. "Come on up. You can ride with me," he said.

Dixie climbed up and sat on the seat with him. "You go to the old pecan grove, Candy. That's where it is."

He drove the tractor slowly. But still it was much faster than walking. All the way, he didn't say much, and neither did Dixie.

Finally they got to the barn, and she said, "Stop over there."

He stopped the tractor close to the old building.

She said, "Now don't be scared, Candy." Then she called out, "Jumbo! Jumbo!"

Candy looked up to see a full-grown elephant come from around the back of the barn. At first Dixie wondered if he'd run as Shep had. But he just sat there on the tractor seat, staring.

Jumbo came up and stretched out his trunk to Dixie. She took it. Then she began to tell the story of Chad and Jumbo to Candy.

At the end she said, "So Jumbo will be killed if someone doesn't take care of him until Chad can get help. Will you help me, Candy?"

Candy stared up at the huge form of the elephant. Then he too reached out and stroked the huge trunk.

"Sure I will," he said. And then he gave Dixie a big smile. "I always liked animals better than people anyway!"

9

DIXIE MAKES A PROMISE

Sunday morning Dixie went to church. She didn't hear much of what the preacher said, though.

After church, Uncle Roy said, "We're going to eat lunch at the Palace Cafe. Would you like that, Dixie?"

"Yes!" she almost shouted. The Palace Cafe was on the same block as the sheriff's office. Quite a few of the church members ate lunch there on Sunday.

Dixie ate very fast. "I'm all finished," she said. "Can I go play in the park?"

"I guess so, but don't get your dress all dirty," Aunt Edith said.

Dixie went to the sheriff's office before she went to the park. When she went inside, the sheriff wasn't there, but she asked his deputy, "Please, could I talk to Chad?"

The man smiled. "It was all right with Sheriff Peck, so it's all right with me. Come along, Dixie." He took her to the cell and said, "Call when you want me to let you out."

"Oh, Chad!" Dixie cried. "Guess what? I've found a way to take care of Jumbo!"

"You have?" His eyes lit up. "Tell me about it."

Dixie told him all about Candy and how he'd agreed to take hay to the elephant. "And it isn't like stealing the hay, either," Dixie explained. "Candy said he'd pay for it himself."

Chad said, "Well, that's lucky for us."

She said, "Not lucky. I *prayed* for someone to help. And then Candy said he'd do it. Isn't that wonderful, Chad?"

Chad grinned at her. "I guess it is, Dixie. But you've got to do a lot more praying. Jumbo's not safe yet. Sooner or later someone else will see him."

He began to tell her about elephants. She found out that the average age of elephants is fifty-seven years. Chad told her how much they weigh. "Jumbo weighs over eight tons," he said. "And he's thirteen feet high at the shoulders. That's big, even for an African elephant."

She said, "And he's smart too." She told him how she'd managed to get on Jumbo's back for a ride.

"Sure. That's the way he's been trained." Then he told her how to steer Jumbo and how to make him do several tricks.

After a while she said, "I've got to go now, Chad. But I'll come back and see you."

He suddenly leaned over. "I don't usually hug girls, Dixie, but I'd like to give you a big kiss. *Two* kisses—one from me and one from Jumbo."

He kissed her twice, then said, "Goodbye, Dixie. Thanks for coming to see me." Then he frowned. "We don't know what's going to happen—but I want you to promise me something."

"What, Chad?"

"Promise that you won't be disappointed in me—no matter what happens."

Dixie looked at him. "Why, I wouldn't do that! You're my friend."

"That's right!" Chad nodded. "It's the four of us—you and me and Candy and Jumbo. We've got to believe in one another. No matter what happens. All right?"

"I promise," Dixie said. Then she called for the deputy and left the cell.

When she got to the park, her uncle and aunt hadn't come yet. She played a little, then just waited for them. *I wonder why Chad wanted me to promise that?* she asked herself. *I could never be disappointed in him.*

But when she got home from school two days later, Aunt Edith said, "Well, you won't be visiting that young man in jail anymore."

Dixie stared at her. "Why not, Aunt Edith?"

"Because he's run off. Got clean away, just like I knew he would."

Dixie listened while her aunt told the story. Chad had been taken to a home for boys in a small town close by. The next morning, he was gone.

"He's no good, that boy," Aunt Edith said. "Good thing for you he's gone. Now you see what he's like."

But Dixie remembered what he had said: *"Promise you won't be disappointed in me, no matter what happens."*

Dixie waited until Candy came in from work. Then she went to his little house and found him getting ready for supper. She told him about Chad. She told him how she'd promised to believe in him.

"I think he's going to his uncle's ranch in Arkansas. Why do *you* think he ran away, Candy?"

"Don't know," he said. Then he said, "But we got to trust him, Dixie. Like he said, it's the four of us—him and me and you and Jumbo."

Dixie felt better then. She said, "I do trust Chad, Candy. And you too." Then she smiled. "I didn't have a single friend a little while ago. Now I've got three!"

"And one of them is a real *big* one!" Candy said. He was smiling too. "I'll take some hay down to him after supper."

The next day after school, Dixie and Candy drove to Jumbo's hideout on the tractor. They fed him some fresh hay. Then Dixie tried the signal Chad had told her about.

She held up one hand and called out, "Hoochie koochie, Jumbo!"

And the big elephant began dancing! Not very well, but he was shaking his back half, and it was very funny.

Candy said on the way home, "This is

easy. I don't see why we can't take care of Jumbo from now on just like this."

Dixie said, "I hope so, Candy. But sometimes things go wrong."

And she was right. Not long after that, just about *everything* went wrong!

10

A MONSTER IS AMONG US

For a week Candy and Dixie managed to go every day to feed Jumbo. But when Dixie got home from school on Wednesday, she found things in an uproar.

Aunt Edith was lying back on a kitchen chair, and Uncle Roy was shouting, "Where'd you put my shotgun, Edith?"

"What's the matter, Uncle Roy?" Dixie asked.

"A monster is among us. That's what's the matter!" He went to a closet and pulled out a shotgun. "And it's a mighty big one too! Broke into Chester Freeman's storeroom. Tore the doors right off!"

"And the Freeman place is only five miles from here," Aunt Edith said. "Don't you dare leave me here alone, Roy Snyder!"

"I got to join the rest of the men, Edith.

You stay in the house. There were all sorts of huge footprints outside Chester's place. We're going to get the dogs and run the monster down. Now, you and Dixie stay here."

Aunt Edith tried to stop him. But he didn't even seem to hear. When he was gone, she said, "I'm going to my room and lock the door. You should do the same thing, Dixie!" She left without waiting for an answer.

Dixie went straight to Candy's little house.

"We've got to do something, Candy," she said. "They'll find Jumbo, sure as the world."

Candy said, "Come with me. I've got an idea."

He went to the barn and hooked up the trailer to the tractor. After he had loaded the trailer with hay, he said, "Hang on, now. I'm going to drive fast."

And he did, too! By the time they got to the pecan grove, Dixie was just about shaken to pieces. She climbed down, and her legs were shaky.

"Call Jumbo," Candy said.

And when Dixie called, Jumbo came out of the barn.

"We got to move him from here," Candy said. "Those dogs can follow his scent to this place."

"But won't they follow where we go?" Dixie asked.

"Not the way we're going," Candy said. "Animals don't leave any trail in water. Do you think you could get him to follow the tractor?"

"I'll try."

Dixie ran to Jumbo and touched his knee. He got down, and she got on his back. "All right, Candy," she shouted. "Let's go!"

Candy turned the tractor around and drove off.

Dixie said, "Hup! Jumbo!" just as Chad had told her. When she wanted him to go right, she slapped the right side of his neck. When she wanted him to go left, she slapped the other side. But soon she didn't need to. Jumbo quickly learned that she wanted him to follow the tractor. He followed the red light on the back.

Soon they came to the creek.

To Dixie's surprise, Candy turned down into it. Jumbo followed. The water was very shallow. They went for a long way down the stream, and then Candy drove out onto dry ground. They went on for a little way before he stopped the tractor.

"You can get down now," he called out.

Dixie tapped the elephant's head and said, "Kneel, Jumbo." When he did, she got off. "What will we do now, Candy?"

"I think we can keep him here," he said. "Look at this place."

Dixie looked around but couldn't see much. It was getting dark. "Won't he wander off?"

"Not after I work on it a little," Candy said. "You can't see too well now, but it's a little canyon. It's got real steep banks on three sides—too steep for him to climb up. We came through the only opening."

"Won't he try to follow us back?"

"Well, if my idea works, he won't be able to." He reached into the toolbox of the tractor. He took out a chain saw. "See all these trees? I'm going to cut some of them down. If I make them fall right across this opening, it'll make kind of a wall. Take this flashlight and take Jumbo in as far as you can. This saw makes a lot of noise. It might scare him."

Dixie said, "All right. Come on, Jumbo."

The elephant followed her, and soon they came to a steep hill. "We have to wait here, Jumbo," she said. "Now don't you be afraid when the saw makes a noise."

She stood and waited while Candy cut down trees. It took a long time. But finally he shut the saw off and called, "All right, Dixie. It's finished."

"Come on, Jumbo." Dixie went to where he was and saw that some cut-down trees were piled on top of each other. They made a big wall. She said, "I don't think he can get out of here."

"He can if he really wants to," Candy said. "But maybe he'll stay until we can find something better."

Candy had piled the hay inside the canyon, but Dixie said, "He won't have any water to drink."

Candy nodded. "Oh yes, he will. There's a nice spring back there. He won't get thirsty."

"Oh, Candy!" Dixie said. "You're so smart!"

Candy stared at her. "Well, now, nobody ever called me that."

"Well, you *are.*" Then she said, "We'd better get back."

"I guess so. They'll be out looking for us pretty soon!"

They climbed over the piled-up trees.

Then Dixie said, "Jumbo, we've got to go. You be good, and we'll be back very soon."

The elephant lifted his trunk and made a low trumpeting sound.

"He's telling us that he'll be lonesome," Dixie said. "I hate to leave him alone out here."

"Maybe it won't be for long." Candy started the tractor. "Looks like you've got to get some of your praying done."

"You too, Candy," Dixie said. "In the Bible it says that when two people pray for anything Jesus wants done, then He always does it. So let's pray for Jumbo to be safe and for Chad to find him a good home."

And all the way back to the farm, that's what they prayed.

11

THE TATTLETALE

For two weeks, Dixie and Candy managed to go out and visit Jumbo almost every day.

Dixie had a hard time writing to her parents. But one day she felt so bad that she wrote them a long letter. It took a long time to write that letter. She started it one night but didn't have time to finish. At recess the next day, she finished it and left it on her desk.

When the bell rang and she went back inside, she saw Ollie Peck standing at her desk. He was looking down at something.

Dixie ran up to him. "You stay away from my things, Ollie Peck!" She was very angry with Ollie.

"Who wants to see your old things?" he said. He sounded angry too. "I just wanted to borrow a sheet of paper."

"You can ask for it," Dixie said. She gave him a sheet, and he went away. Ollie was always picking on her. She was still mad at him when it was time to go home.

Writing to her parents made her feel better. She'd told them everything—about school, and Candy, and Chad, and Jumbo. She put the letter in an envelope and gave it to Aunt Edith to mail.

After supper, she ran outside.

Candy was waiting. "Better get going," he said. "It's getting dark earlier these days."

She told him about the letter.

"That's good, Dixie," he said. "I'll bet your parents will understand. Maybe they'll be able to think of some way to help Jumbo."

Out at the old barn, Dixie played with the elephant until Candy said, "Guess we better get home."

Dixie said, "All right." She put her arms up, and Jumbo wrapped his trunk around her. That was the way he hugged. "We'll see you tomorrow, Jumbo," she said. "I'll bring you some apples."

They climbed out over the trees and went to the tractor. But just as they started to get on, a voice said, "All right, Candy. Hold it right there."

Dixie looked around and saw Sheriff Peck!

He came up to them and looked at the fence Candy had made out of trees. "Well, I guess this is the monster everybody's been looking for, isn't it?"

"Jumbo's not a monster!" Dixie cried. "He wouldn't hurt anybody!"

Sheriff Peck looked at her. He shook his head. "I'm sorry, Dixie."

Dixie began to cry, and Candy said, "Sheriff, all Jumbo wants is to be let alone."

But the sheriff said, "I can't help it, Candy. I'll have to notify the circus. I saw the notice some time ago—about how he got away." He looked at Dixie. "I guess it was that boy, wasn't it? What was his name —Chad? The notice said that the two of them disappeared at the same time."

"How'd you find us, Sheriff?" Candy asked.

"Why, my boy Ollie saw something Dixie had written. It told all about this elephant and where you were keeping him. I just followed you here."

"I hate him!" Dixie cried. "He's a tattletale!"

Sheriff Peck looked troubled. "Well, I did talk to him about that," he said. "To be truthful I talked to him pretty rough. I also took away his new bike. So I guess Ollie feels bad enough, Dixie."

But Dixie couldn't forgive Ollie. "Jumbo will be killed, and it'll be Ollie's fault!" All the way back to the farm she tried not to cry.

When she went into the house, she found Aunt Edith and Uncle Roy waiting for her.

Uncle Roy looked upset. So did her aunt. "You should have told us about this, Dixie," Uncle Roy said. "It's not smart to try to do things on your own. I'm sorry you didn't trust me."

"Oh, Uncle Roy," Dixie cried. "I wanted to—but I was afraid something would happen to Jumbo. I wrote Mother and Daddy about it yesterday—and I wish I hadn't. That sneak Ollie saw it and told!"

She ran upstairs and shut the door. Then she fell across the bed and cried as though her heart would break.

Finally her aunt came in. She sat down on the bed and said, "Dixie, I haven't been very nice to you since you've been here. I'm very sorry. But I want us to be closer. Your uncle and I will do all we can. He says he's going to try to get them to let Jumbo stay on our place."

Dixie sat up and threw her arms around the woman's neck. It was the first time she'd done that. "Oh, Aunt Edith, that would be wonderful!"

Aunt Edith held her, then said, "Well, Sheriff Peck didn't think it would be possible—but your Uncle Roy is going to try."

Dixie said, "If it wasn't for that old Ollie Peck, Jumbo wouldn't be in trouble. I hate him!"

Aunt Edith said slowly, "I think the Bible says if we hate people, Jesus won't answer our prayers."

Dixie sat still for a long time. Then she sighed and said, "Well, then, I won't hate him. It'll be hard to *like* him, though. He's been so mean."

"I know. But if we try to understand *why* people sometimes don't do the right thing, it makes it easier to love them."

"All right, then," Dixie said. "I'll forgive him, and I'll try to like him too." Then she said, "Maybe we better pray again—now that I'm not mad at Ollie anymore. I'll tell Jesus about that."

So they prayed. And Dixie felt much better.

12

JUST ONE LITTLE MIRACLE

I'm sorry, Dixie, but I just don't have any choice."

Sheriff Peck *looked* sorry. His face was sad. He looked down at the floor. It was three days after he had found Jumbo, and Dixie had prayed every day that something would happen to save the elephant.

But she saw that he had bad news. "What do you mean, Sheriff Peck?"

"Well, I've made several calls to the circus since we found Jumbo. I tried to get them to take him back. But they say he's too old for the circus."

Dixie said, "But Uncle Roy says that we can keep Jumbo here. Let's ask them to give Jumbo to us."

"I've already done that, Dixie," Uncle Roy said. "But they're afraid he'll hurt somebody."

Then the sheriff cleared his throat and said, "I hate to tell you this, Dixie. The circus is going to send a man to put Jumbo to sleep."

Dixie's eyes filled with tears. "But they can't do that!"

"I guess they can, Dixie," Uncle Roy said. "Legally he belongs to them, and they can do anything they want with him."

Candy and Ollie were in the room too. Candy said, "We been praying for Jumbo to be saved, haven't we?"

Uncle Roy shook his head. "Sometimes things just don't work out, Candy. Miracles are pretty rare things. They don't come along every day."

Candy got a stubborn look on his face. "Well, I'm just going to keep on believing that God will help Jumbo out."

"Me too!" Dixie said.

Sheriff Peck said, "The man from the circus will be here day after tomorrow. That's all the time there is. Come on, Son. We've got to go. This rain is getting so bad I'm afraid it'll flood the river. That bridge should have been fixed a long time ago."

"Don't worry, Dixie," Ollie whispered as he left. "It'll be all right. Wait and see."

After they were gone, Dixie said, "Isn't it funny, Candy? Just a few days ago, I just *hated* Ollie. But I don't now."

"That's good." Candy nodded. "He made a mistake, but he won't do it again."

The day went by, and the next, and the rain kept up.

Dixie thought about Jumbo all the time.

After school Sheriff Peck was waiting for her. "Dixie, we've got to bring Jumbo into town. Candy says the elephant will do what you say. Will you help me?"

"Yes," she said.

They rode out to the place where Jumbo was. Dixie got up on his back.

Sheriff Peck said, "You just go on into town, and I'll follow."

They started back to Milo. Dixie noticed that all the creeks were high.

They came to the main road and turned toward town. All the cars stopped to look at the girl riding the big elephant. When they got to Milo, Dixie guided Jumbo down the main street. Everybody came out to stare. Many of the children Dixie went to school with called out, "Hi, Dixie!" Most of them said, "Give us a ride!"

When they got to the sheriff's office, Dixie got down.

Sheriff Peck stopped the truck and got out. "Well," he said, "we'll have to chain him to that big tree until the circus fellow comes."

The blacksmith came and put a big chain around Jumbo's leg. Dixie was sad to see that.

A crowd gathered. Some of the people were angry at the sheriff. "You ought to be ashamed, Henry Peck!" Mrs. Freeman said. "Letting them kill that nice animal." Others said the same thing.

But Sheriff Peck said, "It's out of my hands, folks. The owners can do anything they want to with their property."

Dixie stayed all afternoon with Jumbo. Then she had to go home. That night she prayed, "Jesus, the man is coming to put Jumbo to sleep tomorrow. Please don't let him do it. He's such a nice elephant, and I love him so much."

She went to sleep, and it rained all night.

The next morning, she got on the bus and started to school. All day long she thought about Jumbo.

After school, instead of getting on the bus, she went with Uncle Roy to see Jumbo. He was wet, and it was getting colder. She said, "Sheriff Peck, isn't there a dry place for him?"

"Well, I'll see what I can find," he said.

Just then a car came speeding into town.

The car stopped, and Chester Freeman almost fell out. He was shouting something. "Sheriff! Sheriff!"

"Calm down, Chester!" Sheriff Peck said. "What's the matter?"

"The bridge is washed away!"

"It is? I always said that bridge wasn't safe," Sheriff Peck said.

"But it's the bus! The school bus!" Mr. Freeman shouted. "It's about to go into the river! We've got to do something!"

"The school bus? The one my children are on?" the sheriff said. "What's happened, Chester?"

"Part of the bridge fell, and the bus is on it!"

"Come on!" the sheriff shouted. He jumped into his car, and Dixie and her uncle got in with him.

The bridge was just outside of town, so they were soon there. They got out of the car, and Dixie saw that the bridge was mostly gone. The school bus was balanced on what was left. It was teetering over the wild river.

"Look at the bus!" her uncle said. "There's no way to get those kids out!"

"We've got to!" the sheriff said. His face was white. His hands were trembling. The bus could fall into the river at any second, and all the children would drown!

"We've got to pull the bus off the bridge!" the sheriff said. "Look—there's my boy and girl! They're looking out the window!"

"Let's get a big truck and pull them out," Uncle Roy said.

"There's not one close enough," the sheriff said. "And my little truck wouldn't do it."

They stood looking at each other and the bus.

Suddenly Dixie shouted, "Sheriff Peck! I know what to do!"

He stared down at her. She knew he was so scared he couldn't think very well. "*Jumbo* can do it!" she cried. "We can just put his chain on that bus—and he'll save them!"

The sheriff said, "We'll have to try it. Get back in the car!"

Sheriff Peck drove back to town. "Let me unlock him," he said. "Now it's up to you and Jumbo, Dixie! We'll take the chain back to the bridge while you're coming."

Dixie ran to Jumbo and said, "Kneel down, Jumbo! We're going to save the children!"

Jumbo lifted his trunk and gave a loud trumpet sound. Then he knelt down.

When he got up with Dixie on his back, she said, "Go, Jumbo!"

He left at a very fast trot. Dixie held on tight. Soon they were at the bridge. She saw that the sheriff had already looped one end of the chain around the bus.

"Kneel down, Jumbo," she said.

Sheriff Peck put the chain around Jumbo's neck.

Dixie said, "Up, Jumbo!"

The elephant got to his feet, and she turned him around. "All right, Jumbo—pull as hard as you can."

Jumbo leaned against the chain. At first nothing happened.

"Jesus, please help Jumbo save the children!" Dixie cried. And then she felt him take a step forward!

"He's doing it! He's doing it!" Sheriff Peck shouted.

Dixie turned around. She saw that the bus was on the bridge with all four wheels. She said, "Good, Jumbo! Keep pulling!"

The bus rolled off the broken bridge and onto the road.

The door opened, and all the children got off. Sheriff Peck grabbed Ollie and Patti. He was laughing and crying. Everyone was shouting. And everybody came to stand around Jumbo.

"You did it, Dixie!" the sheriff shouted.

"No, Jumbo did it, Sheriff. Jesus and Jumbo!"

Well, there was a parade back to town. Jumbo marched with Dixie on his back. The children all followed. A man took a picture and said, "This town's got a real hero. It'll be on the front page of every paper in the country: 'ELEPHANT SAVES THIRTY CHILDREN!'"

After Dixie got down, she saw a strange man talking to the sheriff.

"That's the man from the circus," someone said.

Dixie ran to stand beside Sheriff Peck along with Ollie and Patti.

The man was saying, "But that elephant belongs to the circus, Sheriff! I've come to put him to sleep!"

"You lay one hand on Jumbo, and I'll lock you up!" Sheriff Peck said loudly.

A cheer went up from the crowd.

The sheriff said, "You might just as well get in your car and be on your way. I may lose my job, but that elephant is going to have anything this town can give him!"

Well, the crowd *did* cheer then.

And Dixie whispered, "We got our miracle, didn't we, Uncle Roy!"

"We sure did, Dixie!" her uncle said, giving her a hug. "From now on, I'm going to trust the Lord when He makes a promise!"

13
GOOD-BYE AND HELLO

Everybody in town came to the party held in Jumbo's honor.

It wasn't the usual type of party. In the first place, it was held in the park outside Sheriff Peck's office. And the guest of honor didn't eat cake and ice cream but bucket after bucket of fresh vegetables!

The whole thing had been Ollie's idea. "Jumbo is a hero," he'd said, "and every hero ought to have a party and a medal." His father liked the idea.

There was a platform with red, white, and blue ribbons, where the band sat. At the head of a big table, Dixie sat with her uncle and aunt.

Jumbo was right behind her. Instead of a glass of punch, he had a washtub full of water. Once he took up a lot of it and sprayed it all over the mayor and the sheriff, but they just laughed with all the others.

Everybody ate a mountain of cake and finished off gallons of punch. Then Sheriff Peck stood up. Everyone got quiet, and he made a little speech. He said, "All of us are wrong from time to time—and I want to tell Dixie and Candy and Jumbo how wrong I was."

He told the whole story about how Dixie and Candy had taken care of Jumbo and how the story of a monster had gotten around. Everybody knew the story, of course, but a newspaperman from the capitol was there, writing it all down. He had a photographer with him, who took lots of pictures. Dixie had to get on Jumbo's back for one shot, and everyone cheered.

Finally Sheriff Peck said, "So I was wrong, but I'm going to make it up to Jumbo. I'm getting on a plane tomorrow. I'm going to the circus, which is down in Florida now. And I'm going to get permission for this town to keep Jumbo!"

A cheer went up.

Dixie ran over and gave the sheriff a hug and a kiss.

But then a loud voice said, "Oh no you won't!"

Everyone looked around.

Dixie looked too, and there was Chad and a strange man.

"Chad!" she cried. "You came back!" She ran to greet him, and she gave him a big hug too. "I just knew you'd come back! And you look so different!"

Chad did look different. He was wearing nice clothes, and his hair was cut. He grinned and said, "Well, Dixie, I heard on the radio all about Jumbo and how he saved the children's lives. Up until then I was worried. I wasn't sure that a little girl would be able to take care of a big elephant till I got back. But I see now that you did."

"I told you I'd pray, didn't I?" Dixie said.

"You did. And it's sure made me think different about praying to God."

Just then the sheriff broke in. "Young fellow, I hate to have to say this, but you're wanted by the law. I'm going to have to arrest you."

Chad nodded. "I know that, Sheriff Peck. And I don't mind. The only reason I ran away was to get help for Jumbo—and I did that."

"He sure did!" The big man standing beside Chad spoke up. He wore cowboy boots, a tall hat, and had a loud voice. "I'm L. G. Taylor from Arkansas. I'm Chad's uncle —and I've come to take that elephant back to my place."

"Why, you can't do that, Mr. Taylor," the sheriff said. "He belongs to the circus. I'm going to Florida to buy him for the town."

"So I heard you say, Sheriff," Mr. Taylor said. "But you don't have to make that trip. Read this paper."

Sheriff Peck took the paper that Mr. Taylor handed to him and read it. "Why, it's a bill of sale from Colossal Circus to L. G. Taylor for Jumbo."

"Right! When Chad here told me the story, I decided to buy that critter and take him home. I got plenty of room for him to roam. He'll have a good home there all his days."

A cheer went up again, and everyone seemed to want to shake Chad's hand.

When they stopped, he said, "Well, Sheriff, I guess you can take me to jail now."

But the sheriff said, "Well, now, Chad, I

just thought of something. We all thought a monster was loose, and we were wrong. And we all thought a thief was among us, and that wasn't quite right either. You only took food for Jumbo, didn't you?"

"Yes, sir, that's all. And I'll pay for that."

"Well—we'll have to make a visit to Judge Henry. But I think—when it's explained to him—he'll be glad to release you into the custody of your uncle."

Another cheer went up.

Uncle Roy and Aunt Edith gave Dixie a hug. "Now you won't have to worry about Jumbo anymore," they said.

Candy was standing close to the elephant, and Dixie went over to him. Everyone was listening as she said, "Candy, I could never have taken care of Jumbo without you. If you hadn't helped, Jumbo would have been killed. And if he'd been killed, all the children on the bus would have been killed. I think *you* should have a medal!"

People had never thought much of Candy Sweet, but now they came up to him, wanting to shake *his* hand and telling him how wonderful he was.

Finally Candy got Dixie off to one side

and said, "I'm glad it turned out like this. But you're forgetting one thing."

"What's that, Candy?"

"Jumbo will be leaving. I'm going to miss him. And you'll be lonesome too."

Dixie hadn't even thought of that. She looked at Jumbo and went over to stroke his trunk. "I wish I could go with you, Jumbo," she said. "I'm going to be so lonesome."

"No, you're not, Dixie."

She turned around to see Ollie and Patti with a group of other boys and girls.

Ollie said, "I wasn't very nice to you when you first came, but from now on you're going to have lots of friends."

All the other children began to tell her the same thing, and Dixie felt very good.

When the party was over, Chad said, "Dixie, my uncle and I are going to leave right away—as soon as we see the judge. I want you to come to Arkansas and visit Jumbo. He'll never forget you, I know."

"I'll come if I can, Chad," Dixie said. Then she said, "I'd better say good-bye to him."

She went to Jumbo, and he put his trunk around her. He pulled her close, and she stroked him gently.

"I guess we have to say good-bye for a little while, Jumbo. But you'll have Chad, so you won't be lonesome. And I have lots of friends now. They say elephants never forget, so please don't *ever* forget me, Jumbo! And I'll never forget you!"

Finally Dixie went home with her uncle and aunt. She was very quiet all the way. They seemed to know how hard it was for her to say good-bye to her elephant friend.

"We'll take you to see him one of these days," Aunt Edith told her.

"Thank you, Aunt Edith," Dixie said.

When they got home, Uncle Roy said, "I'll see if any letters have come."

Dixie and Aunt Edith went into the house, and when Uncle Roy came in he said, "You got *two* letters, Dixie."

Dixie took them. "One is from Mom and Daddy." She opened it and then looked at them with a big smile. "I told them I was sorry I kept secrets from you. They said they were glad I felt like that. They say they may be coming home in a few months." She read some more. "Mom says that I'll get a letter from Aunt Sarah that will have some good news that I'll like."

She looked at the other letter and said, "This is from my Aunt Sarah herself. I wonder what the good news is?"

She opened it and read it out loud:

Dear Dixie,

I have finished my schoolwork. I am taking a job with a circus, taking care of the animals. Would you like to come and live with me for a while and help me? I have written your parents, and they say you can decide for yourself. We will have school together, just you and I, because the circus will be moving around too much for you to go to a regular school. Call me if you would like to join me with the circus. I love you.

Aunt Sarah

Dixie's face was filled with joy. "Join the circus and be with all the animals! Oh, that will be such fun."

Then she saw that her uncle and aunt looked sad. She went to them and hugged them. "I hate to leave. You've been so good to me!"

Uncle Roy said, "It's been good having

you, Dixie. And we hope you'll come back often. But you can't pass up an opportunity like this!"

"That's right, Dixie." Aunt Edith nodded. "And maybe the elephant with the new circus will be kin to Jumbo—maybe his cousin."

Dixie began to jump up and down. "Let's call Aunt Sarah right now!"

That's what they did. And in a few days, Dixie was living with her Aunt Sarah.

Now if you want to find out what happened *there,* you will need to read *Dixie and Stripes*—for Dixie's most exciting adventure came when she became good friends with a white Siberian tiger.